LETTERS TO JANE

A Conversation About Faith

Kevin E. Yates FRAS, ObISB

Copyright © 2021 Kevin E. Yates

All rights reserved.

ISBN: 9798710132401

"Scripture quotations are from The ESV® Bible (The Holy Bible, English Standard Version®), copyright © 2001 by Crossway, a publishing ministry of Good News Publishers. Used by permission. All rights reserved."

Cover photo by Jonatán Becerra

DEDICATION

To Marie, my true north and best friend. And Hannah and Rachel, precious gifts we received from above and released into the world to make it a better place.

CONTENTS

	INTRODUCTION	9
1.	AN INVITATION	13
2.	CHOOSING SCIENCE	19
3.	SCIENCE *AND* RELIGION	23
4.	SACRIFICING REASON	35
5.	FAITH BEYOND REASON	39
6.	SKY FARIES AND SPAGHETTI MONSTERS	47
7.	WHY IS GOD HIDING?	51
8.	DOES PRAYER WORK?	63
9.	PRAYER AS PARTICIPATION	67
10.	THE UNIVERSE FROM NOTHING	75
11.	WISHFUL THINKING AND WARS	79
12.	A BOOK OF FAIRY TALES	89
13.	THE BIBLE AS A LIBRARY	93
14.	THE PROBLEM OF SUFFERING	103
15.	THE GREATEST MYSTERY	107
16.	THE ELEPHANT IN THE ROOM	115
17.	LOVE WAS HIS MEANING	121

INTRODUCTION

We are not supposed to talk about religion. No one ever says that, it is a silent agreement woven into the fabric of society. It is fine to have religious beliefs, but they should remain in the realms of a private hobby. If we ever do break this rule, especially in the context of social media, things rapidly descend into heated battles. Any pursuit of truth is trodden in the mud as combatants become possessed by a single desire, to win.

What might it look like if two people forged the opportunity to have a frank but respectful dialogue, exploring their questions and doubts about faith? That is what I attempt to bring to life in the following pages. It is not intended to change the mind of the hardened sceptic or committed atheist. It is an invitation to anyone of good will and open mind, to explore the objections that stand between them and a serious consideration of the faith that has shaped much of our shared history and culture.

When coming to this book many may ask, "Is Jane real?" To which I would respond, "It depends what you mean by real." That is not to be evasive, but to draw attention to the fact that characters in novels are often hyper-real. They allow the attributes of multiple individuals to be brought to focus in a single person.

This can infuse them with an intensity that is rarely experienced in what we usually think of as the 'real world'. That was my intention with Jane. She is the distillation of a thousand conversations, observations, and encounters that I have had over the years, both in church ministry and as a science communicator.

In the process of seeking to inhabit her mind-space she became mysteriously *real* to me. At times she made me smile, at others she brought me to tears. She even surprised me with some of the things she wrote in her letters. What stirred me about Jane was her re-presenting to me many of the searching souls I have encountered. They often faced the challenges of life without a clear sense of purpose, meaning, or deep identity, cut adrift in this world of infinite choices, but few anchors.

My responses to Jane's questions draw upon my personal exploration and experiences of various Christian traditions. Not all Christians will agree with my stance on some issues, but I trust they will recognise the sincerity with which they are offered, and value the contribution alternative perspectives can make to mutual understanding.

For those coming to the conversation from outside of any church tradition, it is my sincere hope that you will hold off any defensive instinct that might spring up, and permit yourself to engage generously with the ideas contained in these letters. Ultimately, my goal is to help clear a path for an encounter with the One whose meaning is love.

Kevin E. Yates

"In your hearts honour Christ the Lord as holy, always being prepared to make a defence to anyone who asks you for a reason for the hope that is in you; yet do it with gentleness and respect."

1 Peter 3:15

1. AN INVITATION

Dear Jane,

How is the world treating you my friend? It's been a couple of weeks since we spoke at your grandfather's funeral. I do hope Gwen is gradually adjusting to life on her own. I'm sure you will be a great source of support to her, but don't neglect to create space to work through your own thoughts and feelings. I know the loss of parents and grandparents is unsettling. It can feel like our roots to the past are being severed.

Thomas always struck me as a very private man. I never really felt like I got to know him particularly well. So, it was lovely to hear you speak about him with such warmth during the service. The stories you told painted a beautiful picture of a quiet soul, who nevertheless lived a full and meaningful life. It appears he touched many with his thoughtfulness and simple acts of kindness. Who wouldn't want to be so fondly remembered?

Your mother told me afterwards how much she appreciated you stepping up to speak on behalf of the family. I fear it would have been too heavy a burden for her to carry in her present state. We all take comfort in knowing she has you to lean on. Your father would rightly be proud of the woman you have become.

There was something you said to me after the service that has stayed with me, and prompted me to write this letter. You remarked that Thomas was a devoutly religious man, and that there were times when you envied his faith and the comfort it brought him, but it was not something you could embrace yourself. I dearly wanted to explore this with you at the time, but it didn't feel appropriate given the occasion, and I was worried I might appear insensitive, the religious equivalent of an ambulance chaser!

Religion can be a tricky subject to broach these days. It is like we have an unwritten agreement that faith will be tolerated as long as it remains a private matter, like stamp collecting. I find this difficult, given Jesus's instruction to share his message with the world. I do understand people's reluctance to hold such conversations, it can be a divisive topic.

In all of this I would only ever seek to propose, not impose, a way of understanding who we are, and the nature of the human predicament. I hope you can recognise the motivation is one of love, rather than some arrogant desire to be right. After all, what sort of monster would I be if I truly believe Jesus is bread for the world, but failed to share him with others. Don't we all, at our most naked and vulnerable, recognise a deep hunger in ourselves for goodness, beauty, and truth.

This leads me to the proposal that prompted me to write in the first place. Would you be interested in having a dialogue about this very subject? You can share any questions, doubts, or objections you have. I will respond, as best I can, with my own thoughts and understanding. I don't pretend to have all the answers, but I've been on this journey of faith for a few decades now, so I have given a great deal of thought and time to contemplating such things. You can judge the merits of those responses on your own terms. Whatever the outcome, you will at least know you have given serious consideration to the most fundamental of human questions.

You may be surprised to learn that I don't believe that question is really about the existence of God. That is a very recent question in historical terms. The real question, the one we either face head on or spend our lives avoiding, is how we are to live in the world. But more on that later if you agree.

I'd suggest we correspond via letter. I know it's a bit old school, but it lends itself to considered responses, rather than first reactions. So, what do you say? Are you up for this? I'm happy for you to be as direct and challenging as you like, so don't feel you need to pull any punches. And please don't worry about offending me, that will just get in the way of us having a real and meaningful conversation. It's about something that matters, so disagreement is inevitable, but I trust the strength of our friendship to weather any of that. If you want to go ahead, I'll look for your letter among the regular bills and takeaway menus that fall on my door mat!

Do take care and pass on my love to Sam and your mother.

Your friend,

Kevin

2. CHOOSING SCIENCE

Dear Kevin,

Thank you for your letter and kind words. They did bring a tear to my eye, especially your comment about my dad. I do try to live in a way that would make him proud. Giving the eulogy at Thomas's funeral was a strange experience. The responsibility to speak on behalf of the whole family terrified me, so I had lots of conversations with people beforehand. It was an emotionally draining time for all of us, recalling memories and half-forgotten stories. Though I did sense something healing about the process, especially for mum.

I was a little nervous going up to the front, but surprisingly calm once I started speaking. I guess having a task to focus on helps. It was later, when the curtains closed over his coffin, that I lost it. It just felt so final. Any opportunity for last words went with him the other side of that curtain. It makes you realise how important it is to say what's on your heart whilst you have the chance. I've been saying "I love you" to Sam far more often since!

I must admit, your letter coming through the post was a surprise, I can't remember the last time I received one. As you say, it's mostly marketing or bank statements these days.

The rare experience of holding and reading a real letter stirred some feelings that I can't quite explain. So, I would like to accept your offer to 'dialogue' as you put it. I think you've caught me at a moment when I'm more open to such questions. Maybe it's the disruption to the regular routine of life following Thomas's passing, but I do find myself in a more contemplative mood recently. I'm sure it's just some evolutionary instinct kicking in to help me rationalise and process everything.

It is hard to see any purpose behind it all if I'm honest. I get the desire to assign meaning to our existence and to hope for something beyond this life, but it seems so obvious that this way of thinking belongs to a pre-scientific age. In the absence of scientific understanding people naturally told themselves stories to make sense of the world.

Kevin, please don't be offended (you did invite me to be direct!), but given the choice between science facts and religious beliefs, I'll choose science every time. I am curious to understand how you, someone who has studied science and worked in science communication for 20 years, can square this circle. Again, I hope you don't mind me being so blunt.

Your friend,

Jane

3. SCIENCE *AND* RELIGION

Dear Jane,

I'm so glad you decided to accept my invitation. And please don't give a second thought to offending me. I know your heart, and as I said previously, we are both capable of separating differences of opinion from our personal feelings towards one another.

I know what you mean about the weight of responsibility when delivering a eulogy on behalf of your family. That duty fell to me at my dad's funeral. I must say you did a fantastic job. I agree about the symbolism of the curtains closing over the coffin and that sense of finality. I've helped a few families plan funerals for their loved ones. When it comes to the choice of whether to leave the curtains open at the end of the service, I always encourage people to have them close. It inevitably triggers tears, but I'm not sure a funeral has served its purpose if people leave not having faced that reality.

You mentioned the lost opportunity for any final words. That got me curious. Is there anything specific you would have liked to say to Thomas, given the chance? The thought did bring back memories of visiting my mum in hospital back in 1988. It was the day before Christmas Eve, and she had a heart attack following an operation. As I kissed her and prepared to leave, the words "I love you" were on the tip of my tongue, but that wasn't the sort of sentiment we shared much in our family growing up. I also worried it might upset her, and she was already very fragile.

The next morning my brother called to tell me she had passed in the night. Needless to say, it is something I've often looked back on with regret. I learnt from that, and rarely say goodbye to Marie or my girls without telling them that I love them. It seems the most important lessons are often learnt through our failures rather than our successes.

Regarding the science vs. religion issue you raised, you are not the first to question my having a foot in both camps. I get that quite a lot in my job. Especially since I took to wearing a crucifix as part of my Rule of Life as a Benedictine Oblate. I actually don't see any conflict between science and religious faith, providing they are both correctly understood. That, in my experience, is where any issues usually originate.

There are numerous examples of religion poorly construed, and terrible things have been done in its name. In the same way, scientific discoveries, and the technologies they have produced, have often been used in ways that bring great suffering and devastation. In both cases I think it tells us more about human nature than it does about the scientific method or religious faith in themselves. So, let's delve into this perceived conflict between science and faith and see if we can unpick it. This could turn into one of our longer letters, so I hope you've got yourself a coffee and you are sitting comfortably.

Jane, do you remember the Monty Python sketch with several forgetful goldfish swimming around in a tank, continually greeting one another as if they had only just met! It was based on the popular belief that goldfish only have a three second memory. As funny as that sketch was, it turns out not to be true. Some researchers at the University of Plymouth found that goldfish have a memory-span of at least three months. Setting aside questions of how you get grant funding for stuff like this, it does demonstrate how myths can become part of the wallpaper of our lives. The research was published in 2003, but poor old goldfish are doubtless still considered by most to be the forgetful dummies of the aquatic world.

I'd suggest a similar thing has happened regarding the relationship between science and faith. The popular myth is that in the past people were ignorant and unenlightened, so they invented God to explain the world around them. Then along came science and, after a long struggle with religion, finally immerged triumphant from the 'Dark Ages' of religious dogma. As with all good myths, there are strands of truth in this version of events. The example that is usually rolled out is the Italian astronomer, Galileo, who was persecuted by the Church because of his rejection of an earth-centred universe. This story, maybe more than any other, feels like the lens through which most people still view the relationship between science and faith. It's one characterised by conflict and exclusivity.

Sorry to use your own words to make this point, but you said in your letter that you would 'choose' science facts over religious beliefs. I think that illustrates the instinct that is common today. People feel they have to make a choice, are you a person of faith, or a person of science? The Galileo story is complex, and involved personal as well as political disputes of the day. Not that this justifies his treatment by the Church at that time, but it represents just one paragraph, on one page, in one chapter of a much bigger story of the interaction between science and faith.

Far from religion stifling scientific advancement, I would argue that western science arose where and when it did because of the religious worldview. The great pioneers of the Scientific Revolution; Copernicus, Descartes, Kepler, Pascal, Newton, were all educated in Church-sponsored universities. That is where they learnt their physics and maths. And they were all people of faith. I don't pretend to be an historian, but those I have read seem to say the same. One I came across was Prof. John Henry, of the University of Edinburgh, who summed it up like this,

> *"Most of the evidence from the Scientific Revolution points the other way, showing a strong alliance at this period between science and religious belief. Indeed, all the major contributors to the development of the scientific revolution seem to have seen themselves as 'priests of the Book of Nature', to use Kepler's phrase."*

It seems to me that the religious conviction of these early scientists, that the universe was the result of an intelligent Creator, provided the basis for their confidence that it was intelligible. They expected to discover laws of nature, precisely because they were convinced there was a Law Giver. They assumed rational explanations to the mechanisms of the universe, because they believed the universe was the product of a rational mind. As Galileo himself asserted, mathematics is the alphabet in which God has written the Universe.

Jane, I genuinely don't believe history supports the idea that science and faith have always been in conflict. Which has made me question the origins of this engrained sense of conflict between the two. I can think of two main culprits. One is the rise of Biblical Literalism. This is the relatively recent view, among some Christians, that every word of the Bible is to be taken literally. It's not the majority view, but it gets most of the attention. It is this strawman version of the Christian viewpoint that is usually the target of the celebrity atheists. Historically, the Church has always been more interested in taking the words of the Bible seriously, rather than necessarily taking them literally.

In case it seems like I'm trying to revise history to fit my argument, this is what the theologian, Origen of Alexandria wrote in 225AD, when referring to the Biblical creation story in the book of Genesis,

"Who is so silly as to believe that God, after the manner of a farmer, planted a paradise eastward in Eden, and set in it a visible and palpable tree of life, of such a sort that anyone who tasted its fruit with his bodily teeth would gain life?"

Those who do insist on reading the Bible as if it were a scientific thesis inevitably clash with science when it comes to the creation stories. To insist the earth is a few thousand years old denies the overwhelming evidence for the Big Bang and the evolution of life.

I do find it ironic that the Big Bang theory for the origin of the universe was actually first proposed by a Catholic priest. Father Georges Lemaitre was also a professor of physics and friend of Albert Einstein. He presented his theory in a 1927 scientific paper called, 'A homogeneous universe of constant mass and growing radius accounting for the radial velocity of extragalactic nebulae.' They knew how to come up with a snappy title back then! Within the paper he derived what came to be known as Hubble's Law and estimated a value for Hubble's Constant.

Edwin Hubble, whose name is now associated with the equations of the Big Bang theory, published his work two years after Lemaitre, but Lemaitre's paper was in a little-read Belgian science journal, so it didn't receive much attention. Hence Hubble's fame and Lemaitre's relative obscurity. My point, however, is that science and religion were clearly not at odds for a priest/scientist like Lemaitre.

Was Lemaitre a rare exception, an anomaly? Not at all. People of faith have been contributing to scientific discovery and development throughout the history of science. From Augustinian friar, Gregor Mendel, the founder of the modern science of genetics, right up to the present day with scientists like Francis Collins, leader of the Human Genome Project, and John Polkinghorne, former Professor of Mathematical Physics at the University of Cambridge.

If taking the Bible too literally has promoted a sense of conflict from one side, the culprit on the other side is what has been called 'Scientism'. It's basically an attempt to make science the only means of knowledge and understanding. I think we can both appreciate how this view has gained traction. Science is an incredible tool for understanding the material universe. It has been hugely successful, and we have all benefited from it in countless ways. So, there is naturally a strong temptation to conclude that science is THE way to know things.

However, it only takes a little thought to realise the idea that science encompasses ALL knowledge is a conclusion that cannot be arrived at by the scientific method. The claim itself is a worldview, and therefore does not belong to the realms of science, but philosophy.

Beyond the issue of Scientism being self-refuting, it also doesn't resonate with our experience as human beings. Jane, ask yourself what really matters to you. What do you build your life around? Does any of the stuff that you truly care about have much to do with physical constants, laws of motion, or chemical equations?

I think we both recognise that what we all value the most are the invisible things that pass between us in relationships. We've even developed an entire vocabulary to describe these unseen realities: loyalty, joy, gratitude, courage, forgiveness, dignity, peace, honour, beauty, reconciliation, kindness, patience, hope, and love, to name just a few. These most precious of human experiences don't consist of particles or energy. They are the currency of consciousness; the precious gift of self-awareness that flowers in our culture and raises us above the status of mere biological machines.

Think about the weighty questions we might face in life, who to marry, how to respond to the needs of the poor, whether to speak up or stay silent when someone we love is about to make a choice we perceive as bad for them. All these situations require us to look to something other than science for answers.

Of course, we do process these thoughts using the biological material in our heads. Yes, we can analyse this to some degree using scientific equipment, although we still have almost no grasp on the phenomenon of consciousness. But we lose something essential to what it means to be human when we attempt to reduce such experiences down to 'just' signals in the network of 30 billion neurons in our brains.

You are a musician. Imagine what would be lost if we reduced a magnificent symphony to 'just' a series of harmonic vibrations, or a fine painting down to 'just' pigments, oil, and brushstrokes, or a great film to 'just' pixels on a screen, a powerful poem to 'just' vowels and consonants. I think we instinctively know that there is something more to be found in the best art than just the sum of its physical properties. There is meaning, beauty, and even truth.

I think it's possible to recover some sort of common-sense view by recognising that the questions science and religion are asking are fundamentally different. Science is often concerned with 'how?' questions, whilst religion tends to ask 'why?'. Both questions have their applications and limitations. I can explain 'how' water boils from a scientific point of view, but it is also reasonable to explain 'why' it is boiling, because I fancy a cup of tea. Both answers communicate forms of truth, and neither contradicts the other. One deals with material realities, the other focuses on issues of intent, agency, and will.

In the same way, if I want to predict when Mercury passes in front of the sun, I will use science, but if I want to decide if it is acceptable to lie in order to get myself out of trouble, I'll need to look elsewhere for inspiration.

I'm sorry this turned into quite a long letter, but I hope it at least makes some sense. I look forward to hearing from you when you get chance to write again.

Take care,

Kevin

4. SACRIFICING REASON

Dear Kevin,

Thank you for the detailed response to my question! There's a lot to ponder in there, so I'll certainly continue to mull it over in the coming days. I had noticed you wearing a crucifix, but didn't realise it was part of a 'Rule of Life'. Maybe you can explain what an Oblate is? It's not a word I've come across before.

My comment about losing the opportunity to talk to someone was not really about Thomas, although it would be lovely to be able to speak with him again. One of my earliest memories is sitting on his lap at the dining table in their old cottage. I can still smell the mints he used to keep in a bag in his pocket.

It was actually my dad I had in mind when I wrote that. We weren't on the best of terms when he died in the car accident. I was 21 at the time. I could tell he didn't approve of me and Sam. It wasn't anything he said, just a feeling I picked up whenever Sam came around to our house. One day, when it was just me and dad at home, I confronted him.

It all got very heated. I guess we both let out a lot of pent-up feelings, and things were quite frosty between us for a few weeks after. Our relationship did improve slowly, but his sense of disapproval stuck with me and we never had chance to properly resolve that. On some level, that may be what drives me to want to make him proud. Enough! I need to stop now, or this will dominate my thoughts for the rest of the day.

Back to calmer territory. After reading your last letter I certainly feel I have a better grasp of how you personally harmonise your faith and science. I'm still not totally convinced, but I can appreciate that they deal with different types of questions. However, I'm still left with the conviction that science, being based on evidence, is much firmer ground. I'm not sure I could make that leap of blind faith when there is no evidence to prove these matters one way or the other. Seeing is believing as they say. I know that's a cliché, but statements become clichés because they are used regularly, which suggests there could be a lot of truth to them.

I'd like to know how you, a person who recognises the value of reason when it comes to matters of science, can set reason aside and accept a lower standard of evidence when it comes to God. Surely this must involve some mental gymnastics that, in your heart-of-hearts, you know to be irrational.

I hope you and the family are all keeping well.

All my love,

Jane

5. FAITH BEYOND REASON

Dear Jane,

We are all doing well thank you. I'm expecting to be in Swindon next month for a meeting at Polaris House, so we might be able to meet up for lunch if your schedule allows. I'll message you when a date is confirmed.

Regarding your question, an Oblate is someone who feels drawn to the life of prayer and work practiced by monks and nuns in the communities established by Benedict of Nursia in the sixth century. However, due to the circumstances of our lives, such as being married, having children, holding down a job, Oblates simply commit to living according to the 'spirit' of the Rule of St Benedict, but not in a cloistered community.

The journey began for me one day when I was on holiday in Norfolk. I suddenly had a desire (I can't explain where it came from) to learn about St Francis of Assisi. I didn't really know much about him at the time, other than the typical image of him surrounded by animals and birds. I ordered a couple of books from Amazon as we sat in the sun having a drink outside The Blakeney Hotel. Those books were my entry into the world of various Christian religious orders:

Franciscans, Carmelites, Dominicans, Jesuits, etc. This exploration eventually led me back to the sixth century and a fascinating and enduring document called the Rule of St Benedict. I found it a compelling and deeply challenging interpretation of how to live out the Gospel of Christ.

I felt led to include the wearing of a crucifix as part of my personal Rule. It identifies me with Christ in a public way that makes it difficult to hide, even if hiding might be convenient at times. There are Christians around the world today who are seriously persecuted. They are locked up without trial, even killed. Here in the UK, we don't face anything close to that, but identifying as a Christian does invite a certain prejudice from some. People often make all sorts of assumptions about the sort of person you must be.

Part of my motivation is to willingly share, in a very small way, in Christ's emptying of himself. Surrendering of ego (the desire to control how people perceive you) is a strong theme of Benedictine spirituality. The other part is a hope that, as I gradually allow myself to be transformed by Christ's presence in my life, I might bear witness to his love and grace at work in me.

I didn't know about your fall out with your dad. I can see that must have added significantly to the trauma of losing him so suddenly, and at such a young age. I would advise you not to dwell too much on things said in the heat of a disagreement. It's easy to replay those tapes in our heads, but they are rarely a reliable indicator of how people truly feel about one another. Looking to our parents for approval is the most natural thing in the world, but we eventually discover that they are just as human as we are. They are capable of making mistakes, and can easily disappoint us with their own unique mix of brokenness and dysfunction.

As we are corresponding on the subject of religion, I hope you won't mind me saying that I think we are created in such a way that our ultimate sense of value and acceptance can only be realised in relationship with our Creator. That's been my experience anyway. I don't think I've ever told you this, but I was on medication a few years ago to help me through a period of depression. It was partly a result of having a personality that is high in conscientiousness, and carrying responsibility for more things than I had time to do well.

I was already a Christian at the time but, in all honesty, I was very much going through the motions of attending church. My sense of value was far too invested in my performance and achievements, rather than who I am in Christ. I knew this was the heart of the matter for me. The tablets were a helpful bridge, but I needed to find some solid ground on which to stand before coming off them. Looking back, this may be what prompted my interest in more contemplative expressions of Christianity. All I know is that the practice of contemplative prayer, re-aligning myself daily to that central relationship with Jesus, has transformed my inner life.

Coming to your comments about faith, I find it to be one of the most misunderstood words in the religious vocabulary. The fault for this lies firmly at the feet of us Christians. We have done a poor job of communicating it. So, I'd like to try to explain what I, and serious Christian thinkers over the centuries, mean by the word 'faith'. In my own experience, faith has never meant me having to sacrifice my intellect.

Historically, the Church has always embraced reason and welcomed deep and challenging questions.

Faith, properly construed, is not an alternative to reason, nor is it below reason. I would say it is both above and beyond reason. It is what we have left once we have exhausted the limits of what reason can legitimately know. Faith is necessary because religion is ultimately not about collecting information or understanding concepts about God, but a relationship with him.

Let me illustrate this with an example from your own life. When you and Sam first met you didn't really know much about each other, only what your friends had told you. From those comments you could use your reason to assess whether you might be a good match. You may have even Googled one another to learn more, I'm not suggesting you Facebook stalked one another, but it's one possible line of enquiry! Through a variety of means you could gather facts and information and apply rational thought as to whether this person is someone with whom you were interested in forming a relationship.

Eventually, in any worthwhile relationship, things reach the point where you reveal your inmost thoughts and feelings to one another. No one has direct access to this inner world of another person. When they share such things, you have to decide, do you believe them? Reason can point to a track record of dependability, but there is no empirical test that can offer a one hundred percent confirmation of the truth of the matter. When you or Sam say, "I love you", you ultimately have to choose to trust, to take it on faith. You sacrifice the control you have in viewing someone as a mere object to be observed and investigated. You instead embrace their full personhood and move beyond rational considerations into true relationship.

The God of the Bible is not revealed as a mere power or force to be analysed intellectually, but as one who invites us into relationship. The authors of the Psalms in the Old Testament continually use poetic, relational language when referring to their God. "Let the morning bring me word of your unfailing love, for I have put my trust in you.", "Do not withhold your mercy from me, Lord; may your love and faithfulness always protect me.", "You, Lord, are forgiving and good, abounding in love to all who call to you.".

Jane, there are many rational warrants I could share that point to the existence of God, and I hope we can explore some of these in future letters, but it would be crazy to think we could place the God who created the universe under a microscope and examine him simply as an object. Any god that could be so controlled would be no god at all.

God may have left his fingerprints all over the created order, but he has revealed his heart to us through his Son, Jesus. Analytical reason can take us so far, but God's ultimate question to us is, "Will you trust me?"

Peace to you and your family,

Kevin

6. SKY FARIES AND SPAGHETTI MONSTERS

Dear Kevin,

Thank you for your latest letter, and I appreciate your words of support. Our relationships with our parents can be very complex, especially as we get older, and they show themselves not to be the superheroes we assumed they were. I'll try to stop listening to those tapes! It is amazing how detailed your recall of fraught conversations can be.

I'm glad you felt you could tell me about your experience of mental health issues. I think we are living at a transition time in society, when such openness is recognised as a healthy self-awareness, rather than a weakness. That can only be for the good. It's great to hear that you seem to have found a path through to a better place. Finding our value in who we are instead of what we do certainly sounds like a good trade.

I am really enjoying our discussions and find thinking about these issues fascinating. I recently shared some of these thoughts with a work colleague called Darren, nothing of our personal stuff, just the arguments about faith and religion. I hope that is OK. He has more settled opinions on these matters than me and refers to himself as a 'committed atheist'. It has led to some interesting chats over lunch! He can get quite fiery about the subject, but it's often helpful to get another perspective on things.

If I read you correctly you are suggesting that, in order to find God, we need to approach the search on relational terms, rather than seeing him as an object to be analysed. Fair enough, but if this God really does desire relationship with us, where is he? Why is he hiding? Why not simply show himself in a way that makes it so obvious to everyone that he is there?

One objection that Darren raised was how belief in a God we can't see, is any different to believing in any number of things for which there is no physical evidence? He says you might as well believe in a Flying Spaghetti Monster, or a Sky Fairy. A bit dramatic maybe, but it feels like he has a point. How would you respond to that, other than hitting the cheeky scamp over the head with your Bible?

Take care,

Jane

7. WHY IS GOD HIDING?

Dear Jane,

How are you both keeping? Your mum called me yesterday and told me Sam's brother isn't well. She says he has an appointment at the hospital this week for some tests. Do let me know how that goes. I understand we will probably think differently about this, but I hope you don't mind me saying that I will keep Ryan in my prayers. I know from personal experience that having medical tests, and particularly waiting for results, can cause a lot of anxiety.

Your friend, Darren, sounds like an interesting character. I suspect he has been reading Richard Dawkins, given the Flying Spaghetti Monster reference. I think the argument reveals that people like Dawkins do not approach these questions with the seriousness they deserve. It seems ridiculous to suggest that belief in God is equivalent to accepting the existence of a monster made of spaghetti. I wonder if that really is Dawkins's assessment of renowned intellects such as Thomas Aquinas, Catherine of Siena, Francis Bacon, Blaise Pascal, Isaac Newton, Michael Faraday, Charles Babbage, and James Clerk Maxwell? If it is, that is breathtakingly arrogant.

Of course, someone could produce another list of great intellectuals who are atheists, but my point is not to suggest all religious people are smart and all atheists are stupid. It is to demonstrate that Dawkins' attempt to do that from the other side of the argument is petty and hardly grounded in reality. I can only conclude he wants to offer people lazy justifications for avoiding any serious thoughts about God, or ever truly engaging with the real questions and arguments.

If I were to respond to Darren's Flying Spaghetti Monster objection, I would point out that it reveals a fundamental misunderstanding of what serious people mean when they talk about God. Christian teaching is not that God is one item in the universe. Not even the greatest and most powerful item. Anselm of Canterbury (Archbishop from 1093-1109) argued that God is that "than which nothing greater can be conceived."

So, in light of that, it is clear that thinking of God as an item in the universe falls short. I can think of the largest known star in the universe, UY Scuti, but I can then conceive of UY Scuti plus our star, the sun, which would be greater in total. But God, plus all of creation is not greater than God, because creation has its very being *in* God. Rather than thinking of God as one being among many, St Thomas Aquinas taught that God is *Ipsum Esse Subsistens* – the pure act of being itself. God, in Thomas's thought, is the ground of all being.

I once attended a retreat, led by Rowan Williams, at our Benedictine community. He captured this idea very succinctly with the statement, "We *are*, because he *is*." That's a thought worthy of contemplation. This way of thinking about God is rooted in the Old Testament of the Bible. Moses is called by God to go to Pharaoh and demand that the Israelites be released from slavery in Egypt. Moses asks God who he should say sent him if his fellow Israelites ask. God replies, "I am who I am." Moses is to tell them, "I am has sent me to you." This happens when Moses encounters God in the burning bush.

In the story, the bush burns brightly, but is not consumed by the fire. It seems when the God of the Bible shows up, he does not need to displace or destroy his creation, because he himself is not part of that creation. Instead, God's presence makes the bush more glorious. This revelation is in stark contrast to the violent presence of the gods of the other nations with which Moses and the Israelites would have been familiar. Clearly, the God of Israel reveals himself as 'other' than the created order of material, space, and time in which we exist, and therefore he is not in competition with it.

This is, of course, fundamentally different to the Spaghetti Monster, which is presumably made from spaghetti, which must trace its origins back to flour and water, mixed together at a specific place and time. It is also worthy of note that there are no cathedrals or churches dedicated to the Flying Spaghetti Monster, or music, poems, sculptures, or works of fine art. The God of the Bible, on the other hand, has been celebrated in human cultures around the world for thousands of years. The stories and teachings of the Bible have shaped the values and laws of civilisations across time and around the globe. There is clearly something to it that countless generations before us have considered worthy of preserving and passing on.

Finally, if more even needs to be said about this ludicrous comparison, the combined population of those who express belief in the God of Abraham accounts for over 54% of the inhabitants of the planet. In all my travels, I have yet to meet a follower of the Flying Spaghetti Monster.

Your own question about why God is hiding is, to me, far more searching and serious. It is definitely worth wrestling with. You won't be surprised to hear I don't have a neat, one sentence answer. The God I described above, who is the very act of 'to be' itself, is clearly mysterious and will inevitably defy all our attempts at categorisation. That's why we end up in all kinds of confusion and frustration when we think of God as simply a bigger, more powerful version of ourselves – the grey-bearded man in the sky acting as a cosmic puppet master.

The earliest thinkers in the Church were clear that there is something fundamentally unknowable about the nature of God. Christians will sometimes use words like 'being' and 'person' when talking about God, but that's really just for convenience because we don't have any better words to use. This acknowledgement that human intellect alone cannot gain access to God has led to a rich tradition of Christian mysticism. At the heart of this practice is an attempt to draw nearer to God by surrendering the ego's desire to somehow possess God. Instead, we contemplate his mystery.

This may involve meditative reading of scripture, or gazing upon a holy icon, or sitting in an attitude of prayerful stillness. These practices never reveal a complete picture of

God, but they can be a source of light. It's like the contemplative is given a glimpse of a facet of God. The result is never greater intellectual mastery of God as a subject, but an invitation to be transformed in some way by the experience.

If you think about it, the material universe is extremely complex and strange. The old classical model of reality, consisting of billiard ball-like particles bumping into one another, has been replaced by the weird world of relativity and quantum mechanics. There are relatively (excuse the pun) few people who can describe this reality. If you ask them to explain what it 'means' you are likely to receive the response given by Professor David Mermin of Cornell University, "Shut up and calculate!"

In other words, quantum mechanics works and is extremely useful, but what it reveals about the nature of reality appears to be beyond our comprehension. Some highly respected physicists are even suggesting that something like consciousness is the most fundamental reality underpinning the universe. How much more might we have to accept that the ultimate, mind-like reality that created and sustains this weird universe, is beyond the reach of our finite understanding.

Jane, I feel if I left your question there it may seem like I'm evading the issue. So, with the above caveat regarding the limitations of our understanding, I will share some personal insights that have arisen out of my own times of contemplation, as I've sought to follow Moses up the mountain into the cloud of unknowing.

Firstly, there is a sense in which I can conceive of God's apparent hiddenness as an act of mercy on his part. I just alluded to one of the times Moses encountered God, whose presence is usually symbolised by cloud or fire. I think it is worth recounting that brief story,

> *"Moses said, "Show me your glory, I pray." And he said, "I will make all my goodness pass before you, and will proclaim before you the name, 'The Lord'; and I will be gracious to whom I will be gracious, and will show mercy on whom I will show mercy. But," he said, "you cannot see my face; for no one shall see me and live." And the Lord continued, "See, there is a place by me where you shall stand on the rock; and while my glory passes by I will put you in a cleft of the rock, and I will cover you with my hand until I have passed by; then I will take away my hand, and you shall see my back; but my face shall not be seen."*

There is a lot of symbolic and anthropomorphic language here, but let's not get hung up on if God has hands or a back, or we'll miss the author's point. God's goodness and glory is depicted as something so intense that no flawed human can stand in its presence. That can all sound very strange and abstract, but I know from personal experience of following Jesus for over 30 years, that the deeper I go the more aware I become of my own participation in the frailty and corruption of this world.

I've also encountered this in all the biographies I've read of the great saints. The closer they get to God, the more aware they become of their own weakness and failures. It's like driving your car and thinking your windscreen is fine, until you turn to face the sun. At that point, every smear and squashed bug comes into clear view. Might it be that, in his mercy, God remains hidden until the work of transformation he desires to perform in us is complete? Maybe only then will our spiritual eyes be adapted sufficiently to gaze upon the brightness of his perfection?

Secondly, I think we can gain some insight into God's apparent hiddenness by asking what God's purposes are, rather than focusing on our demands for proof. Such demands for God to prove himself do not just come from atheists like Darren, but often, more subtly, from believers too. I've come across lots of Christians with an insatiable appetite for miracles. So much so that they will claim a miracle at the slightest coincidence or unusual event. This desire for some external proof to validate their beliefs dissuades them from pausing to discern if applying the weighty title of 'miracle' is really justified.

Ironically, it is such grand claims, based on feeble evidence, that damage the credibility of the Church to onlookers. It convinces people that it's all superstition, rather than confirming to them God's existence. It also devalues the currency of the authentic miracles the Bible and the Church claim. Christians are instead presented as a gullible crowd ready to believe anything. As I grow older in my faith, I become more convinced that the issue God is interested in addressing is not that we are unsure if he exists, but that we cannot love as we should.

This is a problem of the human heart, and it will not be solved by dramatic interventions from the sky. I think this explains why Jesus often points away from his miracles, regularly insisting that those who have benefited from them tell no one. Why the reluctance to highlight his divine authority over the material world? I think it is because he wants to draw people into a relationship of trust and transformation, not a fascination with (or reliance upon) supernatural power.

God's characteristic way of working is not through impersonal power, but through a relationship that leads us into a steady, subtle, and strangely irresistible process of change. He starts at the very depths of our being, a gentle stirring within, rather than a show of force from outside.

Finally, although God cannot be seen, Christians believe he did take to himself a human nature in the person of Jesus. We don't believe Jesus was just a holy man, or a prophet, but God in the flesh. The Christian teaching about the incarnation is not that Jesus was a human who was particularly close to God, or God just disguised as a man.

Our ancient creeds insist, often in obsessive detail, that he was fully God and fully man. This means God's attributes have been perfectly lived out in another human being. So, by looking to Jesus we can, in some way 'see' God. Or more precisely, we can see what an abundant human life, lived in perfect union with God, is intended to look like.

You may recall I wrote in my first letter that I believe the ultimate human question is not "does God exist?", but "how we are to live in the world?". Jesus is God's answer. Not hidden, but there in history, captured in the Gospels, witnessed to by his followers. And, for those who have taken the step of trusting him, risen from the dead and calling us into a living, transformative relationship today. I'd be interested to know your thoughts about all this.

Please let me know how Ryan gets on at the hospital.

Blessings to you both,

Kevin

8. DOES PRAYER WORK?

Dear Kevin,

I hear you about the Spaghetti Monster thing, it does seem to trivialise something that is clearly of great importance to a large number of people. I do find I am more open to the contemplative side of religion that you described. I struggle with any religion that seeks to impose its rules and tell people how to think and what to do.

Thinking about this brought to mind a visit I made to a monastery near you when I was up in Leicester a few years ago. It was set in lovely grounds and there was a great sense of peace there. They also sold the best honey in their shop. So good that we used it up rather too quickly! I might have to pay another visit to stock up on supplies. Is this the community to which you belong?

Ryan got his results from the hospital and they gave him the 'all clear', which was a relief. Sam and I both thank you for praying for him. Whilst praying is not something we do ourselves, we appreciate that this is your way of expressing concern.

I wonder, would you claim this as an answer to prayer? I'm not being facetious, just wondering how you would decide if what you prayed for was just going to happen anyway. How can you be sure that prayer works?

Something else that has stuck with me is your earlier use of the term, 'rational warrants' when referring to things that point to the existence of God. That seemed like an unusual and deliberate choice of words. I'd be interested to know what you meant by it. Do you have any examples?

Sorry if this letter seems a bit abrupt. I've got a stack of marking to get through! Unfortunately, a teacher's work rarely stops when you walk out of the school gates at the end of the day.

Love to you and the family,

Jane

9. PRAYER AS PARTICIPATION

Dear Jane,

I hope you are managing to keep on top of the workload. I'll resist the temptation to rib you about all the holidays teachers get. I imagine it can be infuriating when people think you have nothing to do when the schools are out.

I believe the monastery you described is Mount St Bernard's near Coalville. They do sell lovely honey, harvested from the bees they keep. They have also started to brew a Trappist Ale that you must try some time. It's amazing! St Bernard's is not my community; I'm connected with the Community of the Holy Cross in Costock. I have visited Mount St Bernard's for a day retreat before, or 'quiet club' as a work friend mockingly referred to it. It is a very peaceful place and there are some lovely walks nearby.

That's great news about Ryan. I am not inclined to claim this as a miraculous healing, but I give thanks that he is well, and you are all spared any further anxiety. I find prayer, like God, to be quite mysterious and difficult to explain. Jane, I'm sorry if many of my responses to your questions appear evasive! That's not my intention. I think it comes from a growing awareness of the limitations of what might be called dualistic thinking. It's the mindset we've largely adopted in the west. We are instinctively interested in 'yes' or 'no' questions. This has served us well over the centuries when it comes to matters of engineering, politics, and the general organisation of society. However, this pattern is less helpful when it comes to matters of spirituality.

The Orthodox Church in the east, and early Celtic Christianity in Britain, both embraced a different way. I'd trace it back to the Desert Fathers of the fourth century. They were Christians who went out into the Egyptian and Syrian wilderness to escape what they perceived as the corruption of Christianity, caused by its collusion with worldly power. They seemed far more willing to live with unresolved questions. Their emphasis was on producing communities of transformation, rather than arriving at clear 'yes' or 'no' answers.

In recent years, I've felt far more at peace with this surrender to the mystery of existence. It takes some discipline to rewire my western mind. I still feel the impulse to rush to a judgement, or a final conclusion, when facing various situations. There is a comfort that comes from a settled position, but the fact that my position on so many things has changed over the years made me realise what an illusion certainty can be. So, I'd rather occupy that tension between the known and the unknown, rather walk the boundary line between order and chaos. It seems to be where the riches of life abound.

Back to your question about prayer. My thoughts have changed as I've grown in the faith and experienced more of life. I began my Christian journey with a very simple model of prayer. We ask God for things and he says either 'yes', 'no', or 'not yet'. I think there is a childlike simplicity to this that makes me reluctant to reject it completely. After all, Jesus once told his disciples that they needed to become like little children if they wanted to enter the kingdom of heaven. I think this primarily speaks to the simple trust we are called to develop, rather than encouraging infantile thinking. So, I'll take that as permission to think more deeply about the practice of prayer.

Of course, prayer comes in many forms, not just petitions offered to God, but I'll focus on that for now. A couple of things we Christians believe about God is that he is omniscient and immutable. Technical language for saying he knows everything and doesn't change. So, when we pray, it can't be that we are bringing him up-to-speed about a situation that slipped past him. Equally, it cannot be that we are trying to persuade him to do something he doesn't want to do. So why are we instructed by the Bible to pray in this way?

I'm inclined to come at this from the perspective of participation. Prayer seems to be far more about what we need than what God needs. It appears, to me, that God delights in inviting us to participate in his plans and purposes, even if we are incapable of grasping the full picture. When we pray, there is a sense in which we raise our hearts and minds to God with the potential to enter into the flow of his divine will. Like jumping into a river and letting it carry you wherever it is going.

Most people who have been on the journey of faith for a while will testify to moments when it feels like God's Spirit is praying in and through them. At these times, the sense of union with God can be very profound. However, I don't want to give you the false impression that this union of my thoughts and will with God's is a daily occurrence.

I must also acknowledge that I have prayed for many sick people over the years, a number of which died, and others got better. One might conclude, therefore, that prayer didn't make a difference and what was going to happen all along just happened. I have some sympathy with those who draw this conclusion. Personally, I am aware of specific events that I am persuaded were direct answers to prayer, miracles even. However, I am convinced that these are never more than glimpses into the fullness of the kingdom that is yet to come. A foretaste of the wholeness that awaits the fully transformed, new creation.

The reality is that we can never evaluate the effectiveness of petitionary prayer via something like a scientific experiment. To do so is ultimately to check if it 'works', and this is to completely misunderstand the nature of prayer. Prayer is not a series of words that contain power in themselves to change reality. That is a magic spell, or an incantation. Christian petitionary prayer, properly understood, is a request within the context of a relationship. Any attempt to measure its 'effectiveness' would taint the authenticity of the request and be a violation of what we usually understand as authentic relationship.

Therefore, we can never know, this side of heaven, the difference prayer might or might not make. Who knows what the world would be like if no one ever prayed? What I do know about participating in prayer is that it draws you more deeply into the lives of those you pray for. It provides a focus for the gratitude that wells up inside when you see potential heartbreak averted, and it can provide a peace that passes understanding when tragedy does visit.

So, maybe it brings me back around to the childlike trust that I started with. Maybe I just gratefully accept the invitation to participate and leave the complexity of how it functions to the omniscient and immutable one who invites me.

Regarding rational warrants for the existence of God, you are correct that I chose those words thoughtfully. I wanted to avoid the language of 'evidence' and 'proof', as today we tend to associate these almost exclusively with the scientific form of knowledge. What I want to explore is more philosophical in nature as it deals only indirectly with material things.

There are, however, things we observe about the material universe that point to the existence of God. I believe they can be powerful enough to warrant a rational person to conclude that the universe is indeed infused with meaning and purpose. The best explanation for such an intelligible universe is a mind-like reality out of which (or maybe within which) it originated. This reality is what we mean by the word 'God'.

One example is the contingent nature of the universe. By this I mean that nothing in the universe ultimately carries the explanation for its own existence. Everything carries with it the shadow of nonbeing. You exist, but you don't have to, and you wouldn't without other things around you, like oxygen, food, water, parents, etc. But the same principle applies to that list of things required for you to exist. Let us take one of them, oxygen, as it is also a component in food, water, and parents (accounting for about two-thirds of the mass of the human body).

We now understand that oxygen, among other elements, is formed towards the end of the lifecycle of stars of similar mass to our sun. This oxygen, from a previous generation of stars, dissipated throughout the universe, and was already part of the cloud from which our sun and planets formed. But that original generation of stars do not explain their own existence either, they formed from hydrogen clouds that resulted from the Big Bang. The Big Bang, the event that gave birth to all space and time, also requires an explanation.

This regression can only finally be resolved when we arrive at some reality that is not dependent on anything else, but carries within itself the conditions for its own existence. This reality is what people have traditionally called, 'God'. There are many other such rational warrants, including the widespread recognition of a universal moral law, but I'm aware this is already quite a long letter!

Love to you and Sam,

Kevin

10. THE UNIVERSE FROM NOTHING

Dear Kevin,

I think I follow the argument about the need to arrive at a cause that is somehow 'uncaused', otherwise the chain of causes never ends. However, I'm sure I recently read that scientists have shown that the universe can create itself out of nothing, which effectively removes the need for a God to cause it all in the first place. Are you aware of this, and if so, what are your thoughts? I'd also be interested to hear more about what you mean by universal moral law.

Ultimately, it still feels to me like the very idea of God is a grand exercise in wishful thinking. Surely the whole concept is just something we have invented to satisfy our desire for meaning, a comfort blanket to protect us from the cold truth that there is no point, no reason to our existence, we are simply here and when our bodies wear out, we cease to be. I appreciate that sounds nihilistic, but just because something is unpleasant to face it doesn't mean it isn't true. Maybe if we accept that, we can just get on with creating a better world for the limited time we have here and avoid the wars and conflicts that religion always seems to generate. That's a point that Darren made the other day during one of our lunchtime chats. He says religion has always been the biggest cause of war and violence. Therefore, we would be better off without it.

By the way, I'm sorry I wasn't free when you came down to Swindon last month, but Sam is away for a few days at a conference in Paris in two weeks' time, so I was planning to drive up that weekend. Would you like to get together for a coffee or lunch? It would be nice to talk face-to-face again. Much as I am finding these exchanges fascinating, it is always in the back of my mind that it must feel like I'm attacking something that is really dear to you. I know you invited honesty at the outset, but it would be reassuring to look one another in the eye and know we are still OK. Let me know if that weekend is good for you.

Take care my friend,

Jane

11. WISHFUL THINKING AND WARS

Dear Jane,

It would be lovely to see you when you come up to Leicester. Email me a time that works for you and I'll make sure I'm free. Please don't worry about causing offence, we are definitely still good. If you like, I'll take you to St Joseph's Tea Room near Mount St Bernard's Abbey. We can pop in to get some honey from the Abbey shop before we leave.

I think the statement you referred to in your letter was made by Stephen Hawking in a newspaper article a few years ago. At the time he was promoting his book, The Grand Design. In the article he claimed the universe will create itself out of nothing.

I have to say this particular book was highly criticised by fellow Oxford professors, including Sir Roger Penrose, Joseph Silk, and John Lennox. They point to Hawking's reliance on M-theory which, as Penrose asserted in a piece in the Financial Times, "enjoys no observational support whatsoever". Others highlight self-contradictory and logical errors throughout the text. The obvious one being that the laws of physics, such as gravity, already appear to exist in the 'nothing' out of which it is claimed the universe creates itself.

I think any reality where physical constants are already in place is hardly what most reasonable people would accept as 'nothing'.

I should say that it was a combination of Stephen Hawking's book, A Brief History of Time, and an astronomy book by Sir Patrick Moore, that first got me interested in a scientific understanding of the universe. This eventually led me to study astronomy and planetary science with the Open University. I later had the pleasure of meeting both these men who had been such a source of personal inspiration. We did a couple of day's filming with Patrick at his house in Selsey, but with Stephen it was when he came to give a talk at the University of Leicester.

I have great respect for Stephen's scientific achievements, but more than that, I admired his exemplary spirit of determination. As you can imagine, I take no pleasure in pointing to what appears to be a blind spot in an otherwise genius mind; one that I find hard to comprehend. I can only assume he yielded to the pressures of the Scientism I discussed previously. I base this partly on his claim in the same book that "philosophy is dead". I cannot help but think a deeper respect and understanding of philosophy would equip people to avoid the pitfalls of flawed philosophical worldviews like Scientism.

Regarding wishful thinking, I would apply the logic in your own argument. You are correct to point out that wishing we didn't live in a nihilistic universe doesn't mean it isn't true. Equally, wishing we did live in a created universe of purpose and meaning doesn't rule out the possibility of that being true. In fact, it seems to be a general rule that creatures are not born with desires that have no possibility of being satisfied. C.S. Lewis makes this point well in his book, Mere Christianity. He writes,

"A baby feels hunger: well, there is such a thing as food. A duckling wants to swim: well, there is such a thing as water… If I find in myself a desire which no experience in this world can satisfy, the most probable explanation is that I was made for another world."

There are other problems with this idea that God is just something we have invented for our emotional or intellectual comfort. Ask yourself Jane, is the God of the Bible the one we would invent if comfort was our main goal? He is certainly not presented as a pushover. He does not let us get away with murder, or any other violations of love. Neither is he portrayed as a nice passive or impersonal God, watching from a distance. What we find in the pages of the Bible is a God that is interested in how we live. He has high expectations for his creatures. Whilst his standards of justice, mercy, love, and faithfulness are all things we can admire, most of us will admit that we fall short of them on a daily basis. It seems unlikely that we would invent such a God to fulfil our desire for comfort; he is just too demanding!

Far from wanting to invent a God to whom we are accountable, what I detect in people is the longing to be free of such accountability. So often, what we want is to throw off any moral shackles and live our lives purely to suit ourselves. In fact, it is this rebellion of mankind against the Creator, and the suffering and brokenness that results, which runs through the Bible like a thread. The goal towards which the Bible continually aims is God's plan to rescue a reluctant humanity from themselves.

So, I don't believe God is the product of wishful thinking. He is the reality to which our longing for the sacred and eternal point. Sadly, our modern lifestyles do not always leave much room for us to contemplate such questions. We must be the most overly stimulated generation that ever existed. In all the sensory noise, when do we set time aside to be quiet and acknowledge the aching caused by the God-shaped vacuum within?

Jane, you asked me to explain what I meant by the universal moral law. In simple terms, I'm referring to our common experience of objective right and wrong. Every day we say things like "That wasn't fair", or "He was wrong to do that." When we do this, we are usually appealing to a moral standard that exists outside of ourselves, rather than just our opinion. We could debate an opinion, such as if toast or cereal are better for breakfast, but no one thinks there is a debate to be had about Hitler's extermination of disabled people. In such a case we all sense a violation of something fundamental, and would rightly deplore anyone who claimed otherwise.

So, the question is, where does this moral law come from? We could say it is something we have invented to make society run more smoothly, but that suggests we have it in our power to reject it or rewrite it. Yet we all have this voice inside, which we call conscience, that tells us some things would never be right, even if there were a benefit for the majority in society.

I find it interesting that we use personal language whenever we talk about our conscience. We regularly refer to it as a 'voice' that 'told' us to do or not do something. If there is a moral law that we discover, rather than invent, it strongly suggests the existence of a Law Giver. This Law Giver appears to have equipped us with the ability to hear this voice, and to feel the discomfort of its warnings when we seek to ignore it.

You (or was it Darren?) also raised the subject of religion and war. This is a complicated one. There's no point denying that wars have been fought in the name of religion. The difficulty comes when trying to identify the motives and drivers behind these conflicts. This is particularly true when religion and political power become entangled. This combination has rarely produced anything positive. However, the same charge could be laid at the feet of ideologies whose roots are found in atheistic philosophies.

On the political right we have the fascists of the mid-20th century and their flawed interpretation of Nietzsche's ideas. They hijacked his philosophical thoughts regarding the 'Ubermensch' (Superman) to justify atrocities that led to millions of deaths. On the political left there is Marxism, which developed under Lenin into the communist movement, spreading from the Soviet Union to Mao's China, and to Cuba under Castro. It is likely that over 100 million people died as a result. The exact numbers are debated, but the order of magnitude is not.

What we can say with confidence is that the bloodiest century in the history of the world was not a consequence of religious violence, but secular ideologies that actually sought to supress religious freedom.

To be fair, I would not push things so far as to blame atheism for these atrocities. There were many complex and intertwined factors at play. I think it is reasonable to request that atheists apply the same generosity and nuanced thinking when assessing religion's part in past bloodshed. Whilst religious intolerance has certainly been an element in conflicts, other considerations such as ethnic animosities, political, as well as economic interests have also played a significant role.

I did a little research and found that historians of war estimate that only 7% of all known historical conflicts have religion as the primary cause. That's 123 out of the 1,763 recorded conflicts. It's terrible, unjustifiable, a grotesque distortion of the religious message, but I think you'd have to agree that the facts do not support the assertion that religion is the biggest cause of wars and violence.

As for the world being better off without religion, it may be a bit disingenuous to ignore the role monasteries played in the development of universities, medical treatment, and the preservation of practically all our knowledge from the classical world. Not to mention the art, literature, and architecture that make Europe such a magnet for people seeking beauty and meaning.

Bringing it closer to today, I can imagine many people's lives being negatively impacted if religious organisations were not there to provide the majority of food banks in this country, or the vast network of debt counselling services.

I am wondering if your friend Darren has had a bad experience of church in the past. Over the years I've often found these sorts of myths find fertile soil in people with a reason for not wanting religious claims to be true. It can help validate their decision to dismiss God. Again, the western mind finds comfort in a settled position. Just a thought.

Looking forward to spending some proper time with you when you come up.

Kevin

12. A BOOK OF FAIRY TALES

Dear Kevin,

It was great to meet up last weekend. Thank you for spending so much time with me and showing me some of the local beauty spots. Mount St Bernard's Abbey was as lovely and peaceful as I remember. That was the first time I'd attended one of the 'hours of prayer' if that's the right phrase.

I can't imagine dedicating myself to the kind of life the monks live. At my more cynical moments I'm inclined to see it as a waste. Yet there are other times when I have to admit finding something strangely comforting about these places continuing to exist. Especially in a world where increasingly fewer things possess a sense of permanence or deep roots.

Anyway, I do feel reassured about our friendship, which you know was a big motivator for me to come up. I suspect it is rare to be able to disagree and challenge one another about issues like this, without it jeopardising a relationship. I find my appreciation and thankfulness for that continues to grow.

We spoke briefly about the Bible when we were driving back from the Abbey, but didn't get chance to finish our conversation. I would be interested to hear more of your thoughts on that. I get some of it, the stories about Jesus caring for poor people and the sick, but there's so much that I either don't understand, or just find too far-fetched to accept. Jonah living inside a whale, the world being created in seven days! What's that all about?

Can you give me a sense of what the Bible is to you, and how you understand some of those bits that just don't seem credible to scientifically literate people?

Hope to talk soon,

Jane

13. THE BIBLE AS A LIBRARY

Dear Jane,

It was great to catch up in person. I'm glad you enjoyed your time with us. Did Sam enjoy the beer you brought back from the Abbey? Assuming you hadn't already drunk it all!

To respond to your question, I know the Bible can be a bit of a stumbling block for many people today, and I can understand why that might be. I've thought a lot about this over the years, so I will try to unpack some of that for you. I'm not sure I can do that in a few sentences, so probably best to crack open another beer.

Maybe it is helpful to first consider what the Bible is, and is not. Rather than a single book as it appears today, it is actually a collection of documents. These individual texts were written at different times, by different people, in different circumstances, using many different literary styles. There are poems, historical accounts, parables, songs, gospels, etc.

I don't want to paint a picture of a random collection of documents that people just threw together over the years. Like most Christians, I believe the Bible is the inspired word of God. But what does that mean? Well, I have a conviction that God has worked throughout human history to make sure these particular documents were written, edited, and preserved. Over the centuries, God has led his people in such a way that they identified these particular writings as somehow special. 'Inspired' is the word Christians use to describe this specialness.

In my experience, the first obstacle that trips many people up when they come to the Bible is asking the wrong question. They want to know if it is true. That might sound reasonable enough on the surface of things, until you stop to give it some serious thought. Can you imagine the response you would get if you walked into Central Library in Swindon and asked the librarian, "Are these books true?" They would probably gather their thoughts for a moment and then respond with something along the lines of, "It depends which section you are in, and the kind of truth you are seeking."

What people usually mean when they ask if the Bible is true is, "Should it all be taken literally?" I've already mentioned that the Bible contains a wide range of literary genres, just like the books in a public library. So, a sensitivity to the particular genre of a book you are reading is important. It is also essential to appreciate that these documents were written in cultural and historical contexts that are far removed from our own. As I think I wrote before, I don't believe we are supposed to take every word literally, but we can take every word seriously.

Let me give you an example. The section of the Bible called Psalms is a bit like a hymn book. It uses poetic language to express deep spiritual moods. In the twenty third Psalm, the writer uses a picture of God as a shepherd leading sheep into green pastures. Is that 'true'? Is God really a shepherd? Are we sheep? Is God interested in leading us into a field somewhere so we can eat grass? You can see that asking if this Psalm is 'true' would be missing the point.

Perhaps a better question would be, "What truth is the writer of this Psalm expressing?" With that question in mind, we can begin to see that the Psalmist is expressing his conviction that God cares for him, and that aligning his life to God's ways will ultimately lead to blessings (green pastures).

A part of the Bible that often causes modern readers problems is Genesis, the first book you'll come to if you open it at the beginning! Interestingly, the opening section of the book of Genesis was very carefully crafted by the author (or authors) to follow a sevenfold structure at multiple levels; seven being the number of wholeness in Hebrew thought. The details are too much to explain in this letter, but I can send you a link or you can Google it if you want to understand that more fully.

My point is that the Genesis creation account appears to be highly symbolic in its literary structure, especially to a reader in the original language. I think modern, western minds can get into all sorts of difficulty trying to impose our wooden literalism on a scripture that is rich with beautiful and powerful metaphors. In fact, I've heard it said that all religion is metaphor, because we are dealing with mysteries that defy simple formulas.

Some truth is best observed in lived out action, or captured in vivid stories that can be retold and remembered. Some truths are so deep and multifaceted that they are best presented as metaphors. I'm reminded how much Jesus used the phrase "The kingdom of heaven is like…" he gave people many different pictures, often derived from nature, to provide footholds as they began to climb the mountain.

Of course, you will come across Christians who insist on reading the whole collection of documents as if they were simply historical, even scientific accounts. But this doesn't seem a reasonable way to approach them when you know a bit about the cultural context in which they were written. It is even less tenable when we observe how forcing a contemporary literal reading onto these ancient texts, creates an unnecessary conflict with the well-established scientific understanding of origins.

I can remember worrying about offending some Christian friends by saying things like this. I still don't go out of my way to offend those who take a more literal view, but I am convinced that such an approach distorts the original meaning, denies the reader access to the truth that was intended to be communicated, and damages the credibility of Christianity in the eyes of contemporary society.

Centuries ago, people got hot under the collar at the suggestion that the world was not flat and was not at the centre of the universe. The Church, and wider society eventually came to terms with those new insights. Today, you would struggle to find a Christian who feels their faith is challenged by the knowledge that our planet is a globe that orbits the sun.

Likewise, the majority of Christians around the world now embraced a less literal interpretation of the Genesis creation story. In reality, I believe this has been a short glitch over the last century or so, when we forgot how to read these sacred texts. I think we are actually rediscovering the original, ancient perspective, rather than coming up with something new.

You may remember me quoting Origen of Alexandria in a previous letter, saying,

"who is so silly as to believe that God, after the manner of a farmer, planted a paradise eastwards in Eden, and set in it a visible and palpable tree of life, of such a sort that anyone who tasted its fruit with his bodily teeth would gain life?"

Origen was not alone in his allegorical interpretation of these ancient writings. Augustine of Hippo and Gregory the Great both recognised that deeper truths were often to be uncovered below the surface of the immediate story being told. If there were any doubt about this being a legitimate approach, it is exactly what the Apostle Paul does in his New Testament letter to the Galatians. He unapologetically interprets two women from the Old Testament, Hagar and Sarah, in an allegorical sense as representing two different covenants.

I used the word 'inspired' earlier to describe the documents of the Bible. Let me unpack that a bit. Even the most literally minded Christians would acknowledge that it was human beings who physically put chisel to stone, or quill to parchment. However, some would interpret inspiration as

God using these people like human typewriters, simply dictating the words to them. I would argue that inspiration is far more subtle than that.

A more informed and mature understanding of inspiration, which better fits the evidence and collection of documents we have today, could be as follows: (1) People had experiences of the Divine. (2) These experiences revealed truths that might otherwise have been inaccessible to them. (3) God, via his Spirit, prompted them to record their experiences in the cultural context within which they lived. (4) God ensured these texts were recognised and preserved by the communities to which they were revealed.

It's so important to remember that the actual words of the Bible are those written by people. People who lived at a time when violent battles were commonplace, people who spoke a particular language, and viewed the world through a specific cultural lens. Yet these words are inspired in that they contain truths by which God shapes a community. At its best, this community is intended to be a signpost, an icon, revealing to the rest of the world what life lived in union with the Creator should look like.

With this model of inspiration, I believe it is possible to recognise the Bible as the Word of God, without insisting that it is necessarily the words of God. This opens up an appreciation for how this self-revealing of God in the Bible has a trajectory. It progresses and grows until it reaches its fullness in Jesus Christ.

The letter to the Hebrews in the New Testament says as much,

"Long ago, at many times and in many ways, God spoke to our fathers by the prophets, but in these last days he has spoken to us by his Son."

Rather than reading things as contradictions, we can start to appreciate them as refinements, or sometimes evolutions in God's revelation. It is like God, in his patience, has gradually revealed more and more of his nature and purpose as people and cultures became able to accept it. We even do this when dealing with one another.

Jane, you know I was involved in church ministry for several years. I remember supporting a troubled young man that I met. His language was foul. He would actually split words up to fit in a few more expletives between syllables! But he was also addicted to pornography, which I could see was acting like a poison in him. So, I ignored the language and focused on helping him find release from this addiction. That didn't mean I thought his use of foul language wasn't something that would negatively impact his life. It certainly made it a bit awkward when I introduced him to good church folk, but I could see it wasn't the priority for where he was.

If we, with all our own failings and frailty, can exercise this kind of judgement to focus on what is needed in a particular time and circumstance, how much more is God able to be gracious and not overwhelm us with all of his truth in one blast! Who could bear to stand in such light?

In the context of bronze age people, when tribal conflicts could easily escalate, revealing a simple truth of natural justice like 'an eye for an eye and a tooth for a tooth' is progress. Whilst that moves them closer to the will of God, the journey is far from over. God's nature is to prefer mercy and reconciliation over anger and judgement.

This revelation comes in its fullness with Jesus, who said,

"You have heard that it was said, 'An eye for an eye and a tooth for a tooth.' But I say to you, do not resist the one who is evil. But if anyone slaps you on the right cheek, turn to him the other also. And if anyone would sue you and take your tunic, let him have your cloak as well. And if anyone forces you to go one mile, go with him two miles."

By saying this, Jesus develops a previous word, which introduced restraint, to its fulfilment as a revelation of God's nature to answer violence with love and forgiveness.

Take care, and give my love to Sam.

Kevin

14. THE PROBLEM OF SUFFERING

Dear Kevin,

I guess it is always going to be complicated for us to get to the heart of what the writers of the Bible were trying to say, given how different our world is to theirs. It is amazing that it has survived for so long, and been so influential. I have to acknowledge that this has made me take it more seriously than I might have in the past.

All this reminded me of when I was studying for my English Literature degree in Exeter. The lecturer was regularly referring to the Bible. One of the students complained that they didn't read the Bible. He told her that Shakespeare did, so if she wanted to understand him, she needed to get familiar with it too.

In all honesty, I have found much that you have said in the past few weeks has made sense to one degree or another. If I am completely honest, I recognised something of myself in your comment about people wanting arguments against God to be true. It would make it all a lot easier!

If it's true, there are just so many questions that seem painful to face. Maybe I'll say more about that in a future letter, but for now let's just put it all under the title of 'suffering'. There's so much pain and violence in the world.

I know you'll have heard this before, but if God is so loving, and all powerful, how can he allow such suffering? I'm aware you haven't been immune to this yourself, with your mother passing when you were still relatively young. And you've shared about your own struggles with depression. You must have also seen things during your years in church ministry that were hard to bear. Didn't any of that cause you to doubt?

This is not a cheap attempt to attack your beliefs where you are vulnerable. I think these past few weeks of dialogue have moved my interests beyond winning arguments. I find myself simply hungry for truth at this point. I've cried more these past few weeks than the last few years combined. I can't explain why. Maybe it's some sort of yearning of the heart to understand how people like you and Thomas can do it; look a world of suffering in the eye and still cling to hope?

Bless you,

Jane

15. THE GREATEST MYSTERY

Dear Jane,

It sounds like you have a lot of emotions close to the surface at the moment. Do take care and let me know if you'd like to meet and talk at some point. I'd be happy to drive down.

I think the question of suffering is THE great mystery. It's the one that has troubled my thoughts for many years. As you suggest, church ministry does bring you up close to some of the most joyous and the most desperate moments in people's lives. I've sat with a father after informing him that his son has taken his own life, sought to comfort a mother as she contemplates leaving her children behind after learning her cancer has returned, prayed with people on their deathbeds, and simply been silently present with a couple as their baby slowly fades away in a hospital bed.

It's all beyond heart-breaking as you can imagine, and the memories have brought me to tears as I write these words. What a pair we are!

The first thing I need to acknowledge is that it's horrendous. It's not fair, and there's no point trying to pretend otherwise. What's more, I don't claim to have anything approaching satisfactory answers.

The textbook response to the problem involves distinguishing between the suffering that people cause in the exercise of their freewill, and the suffering that results from natural processes, like earthquakes, wildfires, and genetic mutations.

It is true that the same natural processes that cause suffering, are also essential for a habitable world like ours to form, and for life to evolve so that complex creatures like ourselves can exist. I'm reminded of the line Morgan Freeman delivers at the end of the War of the Worlds movie,

"By the toll of a billion deaths, man had earned his immunity, his right to survive among this planet's infinite organisms... for neither do men live nor die in vain."

But textbook answers are of little comfort when you are in the midst of suffering. From a pastoral point of view, I do find it helpful to note that many psychologists believe we are far more capable of bearing tragedy when it is perceived as natural. It is the malevolence of others that we struggle to face. It can destroy people. It's one of the more difficult aspects of post-traumatic stress disorder to deal with. Soldiers, face-to-face with someone with the single intent of killing them, are often haunted by this for years. Some also struggle to come to terms with the monster they saw unleashed within themselves in the heat of battle.

Jane, throughout our exchanges, I've tried to avoid abstract arguments as much as possible. I'm far more interested in real, lived experiences, and I wager that's what most of us care about in the long hours of a dark night. I think Dostoyevsky best captured this contrast between intellect and experience in The Brothers Karamazov.

One of the brothers, Ivan, is an atheist whose intellect far surpasses that of his brother, Alyosha, who is a novice monk. Dostoyevsky (himself a Christian) has no interest in presenting strawman arguments for Alyosha to tear down. Instead, Ivan relates terrible and powerful stories of child abuse and torture. It's not easy reading! After his long tirade in which he renounces God, Ivan suddenly looks pale with emotion and asks if his brother will now renounce him. Alyosha says nothing, but walks over to him quietly and kisses him on the lips.

Despite Ivan's compelling intellectual arguments against God, you can't help but leave the novel with the sense that you'd rather the world be filled with people like Alyosha. He is not the smartest character in the book, but he is open to being transformed by love, and displays active love towards his brothers throughout. His mode of being works. And maybe what works and what is true are not so different. Maybe faith is living as if the proposition that 'God is love' is true.

The Bible never sidesteps this problem of suffering. The fullest treatment of the issue comes in the shape of the story of Job in the Old Testament. He is presented as the architype of the innocent sufferer. After 38 chapters that explore various people's theories about why Job is suffering, God arrives on the scene. What is remarkable is that God doesn't offer an explanation, no tidy theory to resolve things once and for all. Instead, God takes Job on a grand tour of the wonders of the created order. The picture that is painted is vast, beautiful, and beyond Job's comprehension.

I think the point is to reveal to Job how futile it is for the finite human mind to attempt to fathom the depths of the eternal divine purpose. Thinking about this brings to mind one of my favourite Rich Mullins songs. It opens with the line,

"Do you who live in heaven hear the prayers of those of us who live on earth? Who are afraid of being left by those we love, and who get hardened by the hurt?"

The song very much follows the pattern of some Psalms in the Bible, which openly complain to God. As the song unfolds the plaintiff, having vented their anger and fear, is eventually drawn to the cross of Jesus.

Here he acknowledges that God has entered into this suffering and shared our sorrow and pain. He starts to see that explanations are not what will help, they won't make it "Hurt any less." At the end of the song comes the line,

"I can't see how you're leading me, unless you've led me here, where I'm lost enough to let myself be led."

In my own wrestling with the problem of pain, I always come back to this point. I can't explain suffering, but I do find consolation in looking to the cross of Jesus and knowing that he chose to stand in solidarity with us, to partake in the suffering. He faced the worst humanity could throw at him, all our hatred and dysfunction, going all the way down into godforsakenness. From that low point he now seems able to gather us up with him and draw us back to the Father.

I've noticed over the years that people who have suffered are often the most resilient. They have a sense of what really matters and are less distracted by the shiny trappings of our consumer society. It has been called 'the wisdom of those who have suffered.' This resonates with me because I do discern a deep pattern of God's wisdom hidden in the cross.

The cross of Christ marks the place where love and suffering intersect. I find it hard to articulate fully, but it is as if Jesus demonstrates a way of being in the world that can overcome suffering, hatred, and violence. In choosing to voluntarily accept his death, rather than fight it, he removed its sting. I find that thought both terrifying and beautiful at the same time. It's an aspect of the cross and resurrection that we easily miss. It's a promise for all who suffer, from the one who chose to suffer both with, and for us.

So, might this world of free will and free processes be the only one possible? I can't access the answer to that using my reason or intellect. Yet, even in the midst of the suffering and pain, I see enough beauty and love that I couldn't wish for it all to be gone. If there were a button that would cause it all to cease to exist, I couldn't press it. I'd rather there be this something, than nothing.

In the meantime, in the absence of answers, I find my hope in the cross of Jesus. I choose to trust that, when our horizon is no longer limited by space and time, we will inhabit the vision received by the great mystic, Julian of Norwich, that "All will be well."

You are in my prayers,

Kevin

16. THE ELEPHANT IN THE ROOM

Dear Kevin,

Thank you for your prayers and your friendship. They are genuinely appreciated. I have found our exchanges interesting, but more than that, they have encouraged me to explore my own inner life. I've discovered things there that I didn't expect. I certainly feel I have a greater grasp of these matters than when we first started this dialogue. I can't say you have resolved all my questions. In fact, you've probably raised more! But I do sense I have a little more ground to stand on whilst seeking answers, if that makes sense? I'm certainly grateful for the opportunity of a frank discussion that hasn't descended into conflict. I wish there were more of this going on.

As you can probably tell from my tone, I sense this particular dialogue is nearing its end. Not because I've lost interest, but I feel we've explored the bulk of the questions, and some objections, that I started with. So, maybe this is the moment to unpack what I meant in my previous letter, when I spoke cryptically of facing painful realities. This could take a bit, so maybe it's your turn to make a coffee and get yourself comfortable!

Something we have managed to avoid so far, whether consciously or not, is the fact that I am gay. I know you have always been very accepting of me and Sam, and she has often commented how comfortable she feels around you. That has not always been our experience of Christians. I feel I should come clean and tell you a bit about my previous experience of church. You see, as a young girl of 12 I was a reasonable flute player. I became friends with another girl who took flute lessons with me, and she invited me to her church. I started to go along regularly, and I really loved it, especially the youth group that met after the evening service on Sundays. They soon became my tribe. That's really important when you are entering your teens and discovering who you are.

I started playing flute in the worship band on Sunday mornings. It was enjoyable, a good outlet for my musical creativity, but it also gave me a sense of contributing something to the worship life of the church community. One evening, there was a baptism service where five people were being baptised. After they had all been through the water, the preacher issued an offer for anyone else who felt ready to give their lives to the Lord to come forward. I felt a fire in my belly, and it wouldn't go away. I had been reading the Bible at home for a few months and praying quite regularly. It was all starting to feel very real to me. To get to the point, I went up that evening and was baptised there and then. It was one of the most joyful moments of my life. So, what happened?

A number of girls in the youth group were starting to date boys. But it began to dawn on me that it wasn't something that interested me. What I did notice, and it filled me with dread to acknowledge it, was that I was attracted to Rebecca, the flautist who first invited me to church. It's not like she was even a tomboy, which might have enabled me to dismiss it as confused feelings, she was as feminine as they come. Long blonde hair, striking cheekbones, my type as it turns out; you've met Sam!

I felt there must be something wrong with me. I was convinced I must be a pervert or something. I tried to put it out of my mind, but denial is a difficult state to maintain. One night in the youth group we broke into small groups to pray for one another. The six in our group took it in turns sharing what we would like the others to pray for. As it got close to my turn, I could sense this weight pressing down on me. Could I tell them? When Hayley, who was leading our group, asked me if there was anything I wanted them to pray for, I just broke down. I couldn't gather myself for several minutes, it was proper 'ugly' crying!

Eventually, Hayley took me to one side with another leader and I spilt my heart out to them. In fairness, they listened calmly and were very supportive. Over the next few weeks, I agreed to let some of my closest friends in the group know what I was going through. A number of them offered to meet and pray with me. We did that, but it made me feel very uncomfortable. The words they used made it clear that they thought there was something evil in me. Something that needed to be destroyed or driven away. I was young, but I was confident enough to remove myself from a situation that I felt in my bones wasn't right. I got up and walked out.

Over the coming weeks people were different with me. There was a barrier between us. Some even spoke directly to me and said if I didn't change, I was at risk of going to hell!

The breaking point came when the youth leader took me to one side after a service and said they didn't feel it was right for me to continue to play in the band, given the 'circumstances'. I was welcome to continue to come to church, but it wasn't seen as appropriate for me to be up front.

I held myself together until I got outside, but cried all the way home. That was the last time I set foot inside that, or any other church, apart from weddings, christenings, and funerals. So, maybe it is me, not Darren, who wants these arguments against God to be true. What's the alternative? If there is a God, if those warm feelings I got when praying and reading the Bible were real, what hope is there for me. I think we both know where I'd be heading.

Yours, a little conflicted!

Jane

17. LOVE WAS HIS MEANING

Dear Jane,

Your last letter didn't make for easy reading. It sent me through a gauntlet of emotions, from anger at the way you were treated, to sorrow thinking of the hurt you endured. Where to start?

The Apostle Paul uses various metaphors to describe the nature of Church. One of his most famous is the human body. He wants the followers of Jesus to think of themselves as participating in an organism, not an organisation. We've lost that perspective to a large extent, and are worse off for it.

Anyway, his point is that we are connected in a mystical way. You can read it for yourself in 1 Corinthians 11 if you still have a Bible. Paul goes so far as to see this union between the members of Christ's body as linking them to one another's experiences. He says, "If one member suffers, all suffer together; if one member is honoured, all rejoice together."

I want to apply that same logic to what happened to you. If one member rejects and hurts someone, all need to take responsibility for that. So, for what it's worth, I want to apologise for the awful way you were treated. It was shameful.

There is part of me that would like to leave it there for fear that anything else I say might risk diluting the sincerity with which that apology is offered. However, I sense there is a deeper concern in your letter, and it doesn't seem fair to leave that hanging.

You will doubtless be aware that matters of human sexuality are currently dominating many churches around the world. I find this frustrating, not that there aren't discussions to be had, reforms to be undertaken, and concerns to be addressed, but because the focus it is drawing is totally out of proportion with what we find in the Bible. Jesus said nothing about it, and St Paul only wrote a handful of verses that some interpret as relevant to this question. So, the high level of concern some have for what other consenting adults do in the privacy of their bedrooms seems out of step with the Gospel of Jesus. Maybe it is inevitable. Rowan Williams once said,

"You can read a good deal of the history of the Church as a sustained attempt to police one another's relationship with God."

In responding to what I sense is in your heart, I think it best to approach it from a variety of perspectives. I will not be engaging with the usual highly polarised arguments that quickly descend into people from different camps shouting across one another. I hope you'll stick with me as I attempt to occupy the thought-space of various perspectives and seek to represent them fairly.

My starting point would be to remove religion, or any value system from the question, and try to establish a purely biological picture of human sexual activity. This will inevitably produce a cold, dispassionate, laboratory-like image. It will fall short of capturing the fullness and complexity of human relationships, but I think it could act as a reasonable foundation stone on which to build before we enter the more biased and greyer world of human values and judgements.

It is hard to deny that if an alien species visited our planet and abducted a male and female human specimen to examine, they would conclude that male genitalia have evolved to deliver sperm to the ovaries of the female, with the purpose of producing offspring and continuing the species. They would recognise a complementarity to the male and female organs. So far, so obvious.

Now, before we leave this, admittedly inadequate assessment of human sexual function, I think it is helpful to identify a fundamental difference in the assumptions out of which the secular and the religious mind operate. Back in the fourth century BC, Aristotle defined four lines of investigation required to truly 'know' something. He called them Causes. The Material Cause, which seeks to know the stuff out of which something is made, the Formal Cause, which focuses on the shape of the thing, the Efficient Cause that tries to uncover the origins of the thing, and the Final Cause, which asks questions about its purpose.

Aristotle's Doctrine of Causes shaped western thinking for centuries, and is still hugely influential today. However, starting with the Enlightenment, the secular mind has increasingly focused on the Material, Formal, and (to a lesser extent) Efficient Causes. It is no coincidence that these are the sorts of questions science is geared to answer. Questions of Final Cause, the purpose of a thing, have fallen out of fashion. And this is the dividing point.

The religious mind, with its conviction that the universe is the created product of a mind-like reality, is still very interested in the purpose and meaning of things. The secular mind, working out of the conviction that the universe is simply here, assumes any sense of purpose or meaning is something we have constructed. For them, such subjective attempts to manufacture meaning may be helpful for individuals, or even whole societies, but they come from within us, and we therefore have the right to change or reject them if we so choose. For the religious mind, meaning comes from without, from God. We discover it, we do not construct it, so we do not have the right to change it.

With these different assumptions in mind, it is easier to understand the thinking that underpins the Roman Catholic position on human sexuality. It has traditionally seen the primary 'purpose' of the sexual act as reproduction. In more recent years it has acknowledged the important role of sexual intimacy and pleasure in strengthening the bond between a couple, but still considers something amiss if sexual expression is ever closed to the possibility of reproducing life. Hence this church's ban on masturbation, marriage of someone who is medically impotent, same sex relationships, and contraception.

Whilst I find the internal logic of this reasonable, it does seem, to me, quite a narrow and restricted understanding of human sexuality. It is also not without its negative consequences on the marriages of those Catholics who try to abide by the teaching. Surveys show that, in practice, a large number of Catholics simply ignore it and use contraception.

I do believe some sincerely hold the belief that sex should not be separated from its purpose of reproduction, which makes me reluctant to use labels like 'homophobic' to characterise them. It feels like a lazy and inaccurate summary of their motivations. It moves us quickly from rational argument to personal attack, which ends the conversation. Of course, there is no shortage of others whose views are shaped by a mean or hateful spirit, for which the label might be more appropriate.

Following the Reformation, some strands within protestant Christianity developed a more relaxed attitude towards sex. This was due in large part to Martin Luther's theology of the body, which grew out of his thinking about the implications of the incarnation of Christ in a physical, sensory body. A few centuries on, this has resulted in the widespread acceptance of contraception among the majority of protestant churches. With this comes the implicit acceptance of separating the sexual act from any sincere openness to reproduction. Thus, pleasure and intimacy become satisfactory goals in themselves. I'm not convinced many protestants are consciously aware of this subtle move from tradition. I suspect it is just an unspoken assumption for most.

It needs to be acknowledged that this changes the picture when it comes to protestant objections to same sex partnerships. The argument can no longer be strictly about purpose. If you recognise pleasure and intimacy as legitimate goals in themselves, what is the rationale for denying same sex couples those experiences? What remains is the appeal to the complementarity between the male and female 'form'. It is an argument based on nature. Put simply, male and female literally fit together. Of course, I doubt many heterosexual Christian couples limit their nocturnal activities to those involving this specific complementarity. That could be an uncomfortable survey to conduct!

Rather than appealing to rational arguments involving any of Aristotle's Causes, most protestant Christians who object to same sex relationships appeal instead to the Bible as their authority. It always triggers my radar when I see the words 'authority' and 'Bible' in the same sentence. I sense it means we are back to policing one another again, which I don't think is the purpose of the Bible. I'm more comfortable seeing it as a pillar, along with reason and tradition. It provides light to guide us in our spiritual journey, both as individuals and as communities. It just always seems to work better when the focus is on how it can challenge and transform me from within, rather than me becoming obsessed with how I think it should transform others.

I'm much more inclined to encourage individuals and communities to engage in a living relationship with Jesus, and trust him to transform people where and when he knows they need it most. That will no doubt include our sexual wellbeing, whatever the orientation of our attraction.

The bottom line is that Christians have interpreted the Bible as teaching against same sex relationships for the vast majority of the history of the Church. Of course, there have been large periods of history when the same could be said about the earth being flat, and slavery playing an acceptable role in economics. So, persistence of a particular biblical interpretation is no guarantee of its validity.

I would contend that it is a sincere belief among many Christians that the Bible does teach against same sex relations. For them, rejecting that would be seen as capitulating to cultural pressures. It would be, in their eyes, an act of unfaithfulness towards God. So, once again, labelling such people as 'homophobic' doesn't really reflect their motivation. It's not that they hate, or are fearful (which is what the word means) of gay people. They genuinely believe it is not in their gift to change what they believe God has ordained.

I still think it is reasonable to ask such people to focus on their own need for transformation into the image of Christ, and trust God to work to his priorities in the lives of others. However, when people start to discriminate, reject, limit participation, or act out of anything but love for the other, something has gone wrong, and it needs to be condemned.

When it comes to what the Bible actually says, there is very little in the New Testament. I will stick with this because extracting which laws of the Old Testament are to be carried over into the Church era seems to miss the whole point of what Christ ushered in. His kingdom is about living under grace, not law. Jesus sums up the whole law as ultimately being about loving God and loving one another. Of course, love isn't about emotional feelings, though it often stirs them. Love is about seeking the good of the other purely for their sake, and not to achieve any of my own goals. That may include guiding people away from destructive behaviours as well as towards positive ones, but it is never about getting my way.

St Paul, who wrote most of the New Testament letters, and all the text that are used in discussions about sexuality, called Christians to a life of union with Christ. He uses some version of the formula, 'in Christ' over 200 times. He encourages them to surrender ego, and submit themselves to the prompting of the Holy Spirit. That prompting and guidance often comes when reading the scriptures with openness and humility. Paul does give some specific examples of behaviour that is not in keeping with being 'in' Christ, but these seem to act like crash barriers on a motorway, rather than laws. They are there as a precaution to stop us going way off course. Basically, if you are doing some of this stuff, Paul says, you might want to re-evaluate your practice of listening to God's voice. It's a warning sign that kingdom living isn't taking root in you.

Among the practices that Paul lists is a Greek word, 'arsenokoitēs'. It doesn't appear in Greek writing until Paul's use of it in his letters to the Corinthians and to Timothy. Up until 1946 this word was translated in a way that implied sexual exploitation of young boys. Given the culture within which Paul was writing, and the widespread practices of both temple prostitution and general paederasty in the Roman world, this seems likely what Paul had in mind.

It was only with the publication of the Revised Standard Version of the Bible in 1946 that the word was translated as 'homosexuality'. The other place where Paul has been interpreted as condemning same sex relations is in his letter to the Romans. The context is Paul painting a picture of the pagan world rejecting what creation could teach them about God, and so being given over to various practices.

I won't pretend there aren't arguments about how to translate and interpret these texts. I've struggled with these myself over the years. I've questioned if I was wanting to pick the route of least resistance, to 'capitulate to cultural pressure'. But that didn't ring true, as adopting a more inclusive stance actually made me less popular with some in my church circles. I have actually been unfriended by a few people! Inclusivity also felt like a genuine response of love in the face of cruelty and ignorance. Being in this liminal space was mental torture, until I felt God speak to me very clearly and say, "If in doubt, love." It wasn't an audible voice, but something that came up from deep within during a time of prayer. It produced peace and joy, which are always good indicators that it's heavenly in its origin.

Another turning point came when I got to know several Christians who are gay. In the same way that travel to different cultures challenges your assumptions, and what you've been conditioned to perceive as normal, getting to know these people opened me in a way that nothing else could. I observed them serving God and loving people. I recognised in them the same faith that flowed in my spiritual veins. I became friends with one particular person, an Orthodox Christian. We would meet up for Evening Prayer at the Cathedral occasionally and go for a meal afterwards. We had long, fruitful conversations. During one such discussion he told me a similar story to yours about a painful experience in church as a young man. He also told me how when he reads St Paul, he doesn't recognise himself in that list of out of control, depraved people. I would add that I don't recognise him in that description either. Nor does it describe what I know of you and Sam.

A real moment of epiphany came for me one morning as I was driving to meet with my Spiritual Director. These arguments were continuing to rattle around in my head, and I still wondered occasionally if I was convincing myself of a particular viewpoint because it was what I wanted to believe. I prayed desperately that God would make it clear to me one way or the other. As I pulled out of a built-up area into open countryside, a bright rainbow filled the sky in front of me. The contemporary association of this symbol with LGBT rights did not escape me! I felt a peace descending on me as I continued to drive towards Launde Abbey.

Jane, the bottom line for me is that I am convinced same sex attraction is not a choice. I've heard too many stories of people who have suffered as a result, it is just not credible that anyone would choose that. To say it is a choice would also suggest that I could choose it if I wanted, which I know not to be the case. The reality I can't deny is that around 2.2 percent of the adult UK population (according to the latest government statistics), are gay. So, for me, as a Christian, the real question is what does the love of Jesus look like in my response to that? It certainly doesn't look like kicking someone out of the worship band. It doesn't look like telling someone they are going to hell. It doesn't look like pressure to deny a core element of your identity or risk being rejected by your tribe.

Everything I've experienced of Jesus over the decades tells me to affirm that you are a beloved child of God. I would encourage you, if you are able, to draw a distinction between the loving God who created you, and his flawed representatives on earth. My prayer is that you rediscover the fire that burned in you when you first opened yourself to Jesus as that young flute player. I pray you can find peace in his acceptance of you in your naked reality, not feeling you have to pretend to be anyone you are not.

We all carry scars this life has inflicted on us. My experience is that they can be redeemed in his presence. He can take what makes us feel weak and turn it into strength. He has a way of transfiguring death into resurrection, it's all part of that deep pattern of his wisdom.

Jane, let's meet up to talk in person again soon.

God bless,

Kevin

ABOUT THE AUTHOR

Kevin studied theology at Springdale College, Birmingham, and was ordained as a Minister in the Fellowship of the Churches of Christ in Great Britain and Ireland in 1993. He has over 30 years' experience of preaching and leading worship in both Evangelical and Charismatic/Anglo-Catholic churches.

He has a BSc from the Open University where he studied Astronomy and Planetary Science. He was elected as a Fellow of the Royal Astronomical Society in 2002. For ten years he managed the UK government's Near Earth Object Information Centre, based at the National Space Centre in Leicester, where he also served as Space Communications Manager.

Kevin has conducted hundreds of TV and radio interviews covering a wide range of topics, including the perceived conflict between faith and science. He has also authored scripts for award-winning full-dome planetarium shows narrated by actors such as David Tennant and Rupert Grint. These shows have played in over 600 planetaria across 60 countries.

Today, Kevin works as the Head of Exhibitions at the National Space Centre. He is a Benedictine Oblate of The Community of the Holy Cross, Costock, UK.

Printed in Great Britain
by Amazon